This book belongs to

....

D1315429

Note to parents or carers:

There are a number of therapeutic techniques used in this book that are designed to help your child fall asleep. Empathizing with reasons your child might not be ready to sleep relieves anxiety and helps calm the mind. Pointing out how each animal settles down leads your child through a visualization that will help relax the body. Repeating key words introduces a gentle rhythm that is slightly meditative and induces a sleepy state.

As you read, keep your voice calm and steady, putting emphasis on the repetitive words and phrases in bold. Add actions to some of the suggestions, such as yawning and breathing deeply. The resonance with your bodily state should soothe your child, helping him or her to feel more relaxed. If your child is not sleepy enough for bed by the end of the book, read it again.

We hope that by combining this book with a calm environment and confident bedtime routine, you and your child can develop an enjoyable bedtime experience together.

This edition published by Parragon Books Ltd in 2016 and distributed by

Parragon Inc.
440 Park Avenue South, 13th Floor
New York, NY 10016
www.parragon.com

Copyright © Parragon Books Ltd 2013-2016

Written by Claire Hawcock, MA and Diploma in Humanistic and Integrative Psychotherapy
Illustrated by Charlotte Cooke

ISBN 978-1-4748-5253-1

Printed in China

Read
Me to
Sleep

PaRragon

Bath • New York • Cologne • Melbourne • Delhi
Hong Kong • Shenzhen • Singapore

After each day ends and night falls,
It's time to go to bed.

When moon and stars fill up the sky,
It's time to go to sleep.

But sometimes when **you want to sleep**,
Lightning streaks across the sky,
Strong winds blow through creaking trees,
And rain beats down on to the leaves.

So, even though **you want to sleep**,
It's hard to settle down.

Yes, sometimes when **you want to sleep,**
But aren't yet ready to close your eyes,
It's hard to settle down.

So first, before you go to bed,
Let's say good night to friends.

Look how Pony slumbers, on her clover lawn.
The grass is soft; she's breathing deeply.
"Good night, Pony.
Sleep tight. Sweet dreams.
Sleep, Pony, sleep."

See how Squirrel curls her tail,
wrapping up warm.
The tree is cozy; she's breathing deeply.
"Good night, Squirrel.
Sleep tight. Sweet dreams.
Sleep, Squirrel, sleep."

Look as Owl's big round eyes, slowly, slowly shut.
The hollow is dark; he's breathing deeply.
"Good night, Owl.
Sleep tight. Sweet dreams.
Sleep, Owl, sleep."

See the birds yawn widely. Yaaawwwn!

And Mouse, breathing slowly—first in … then out …

"Good night, my friends.
**Sleep tight. Sweet dreams.
Sleep, my friends, sleep.**"

Now here at home it's bedtime.
Your turn to go to sleep.

Your bed is cozy; you're breathing deeply.
Soon you'll **be fast asleep.**

Curl up and snuggle down,
Yaaawwwn and close those sleepy eyes.

Be safe, be warm,
Breathe in … then out …

Good night, good night.
Sleep tight. Sweet dreams.

Sleep, sleep, sleep.